Clarence Goes Out West and Meets a Purple Horse

written and illustrated by Jean Ekman Adams

rising moon

To my family,
and to Smoky and Clarence.

With thanks to Taylor.

Clarence is going on a trip. He packs very carefully.

Clarence is going Out West on a bus and he is going to stay at a ranch. Then he is going to come home again. He has it all planned.

Clarence loves the bus.
He looks out the window.

He peeks
under the seat.

He reclines.

He has a
few snacks.

After a very long ride, the bus arrives Out West. Clarence sees his first cactus. The West is very big—lots of mountains and lots of sky.

Clarence arrives at the ranch too late for dinner. He doesn't know anybody, his stomach is empty, and he just remembers he forgot to bring his favorite pillow. Clarence feels a little homesick.

That first night, Clarence has trouble falling asleep, even though he is wearing his cloud hat.

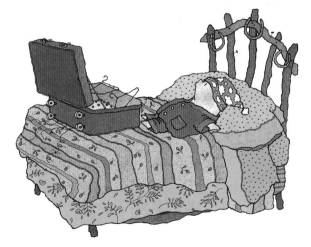

Early the next morning, Clarence has seven flapjacks, two orange peels, a biscuit, and four corn cobs for breakfast. Ranch food is good. Clarence feels bouncy.

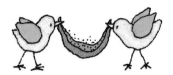

Clarence trots down to the corral to see the ranch horses. He is very excited. Up close, they are quite tall. Their legs look like tree trunks.

One horse snorts right on Clarence's face and says, "Howdy! I am Smoky and I am going to be your horse this week. I will teach you to ride and wrangle and jingle your spurs on Saturday night!"

Clarence backs up two pig steps. He feels small.

"Howdy!" Clarence squeaks bravely.

Smoky is good on his word. He teaches Clarence to ride. He takes him to the top of a mountain and stands very still while Clarence snaps pictures.

He takes him to the bottom of a canyon
where they have a little siesta.

Later, Smoky takes Clarence to a party and they go line dancing.

Smoky even teaches Clarence how to play cards.

On Saturday night, Clarence learns to
play the washtub in a cowboy band.

Riding can be very dusty. After a long day, Clarence and Smoky take a bath. Life on a ranch is good, Clarence decides.

Clarence is amazed to learn that Smoky can even read. One night, Smoky stops in the middle of a book. "What is the matter?" Clarence asks, anxious to get on with the story.

Smoky looks sad. "The ranch is going to sell me. You might not have noticed, but I am not a young horse. I will not be able to go riding with you anymore, Clarence."

Clarence is horrified. He never noticed that Smoky was old. "But what will happen to you, Smoky? Where will you go?"

"Maybe to another ranch. Or down the road. Over the hill. I don't really know where old horses go. I hope it is someplace where I can still feel the breeze in my mane and the raindrops on my ears." Smoky looks far away.

Clarence thinks about his nice apartment back in the city. He thinks about the pillow he left behind. He thinks about his bus money for the trip home. He thinks and he thinks. He thinks about Smoky going over the hill.

"Goodnight, Smoky," Clarence says.

In the morning, Clarence uses all his bus
money to buy Smoky from the ranch.

Clarence will just have to ride
Smoky all the way home.

It might take a long time.
Maybe years.

But maybe they can stop on
the way to take pictures…

…or to play cards. Or maybe they will join a rodeo.

Clarence the Line Dancing Pig and His Famous Purple Horse Smoky. That would be good.

Maybe they can sleep out under the stars and look for the Big Dipper. That would be good, too.

Maybe Clarence won't be needing his pillow, after all.

Jean Ekman Adams grew up in the studio of her artist father, Stan Ekman, watching him paint from the time she was big enough to hang over the back of his chair. Her father encouraged Jean's artistic talents at an early age. Jean went on to get her degree in English with an emphasis in writing children's books from Arizona State University, but didn't begin painting or writing professionally until much later. Again with her father's encouragement, Jean began exhibiting her artwork in a Scottsdale gallery twenty-nine years ago. She has been exhibiting her art in galleries and shows across the U. S. ever since.

About three years ago, Jean painted a series of

posters about a pig named Clarence and his purple horse Smoky. People kept asking Jean, "Is this a book?" and eventually she decided to make it one. So, she wrote the story of Clarence and Smoky, which has turned into her first picture book. The character, Smoky is based on the real rescued horse of the same name, who now resides peacefully in Tucson, Arizona, where he can feel the breeze in his mane and the raindrops on his ears.

The real Smoky.

Jean lives in Paradise Valley, Arizona with her husband, their son, their two rescued Chinese pugs, two rescued cats, a mule, and a horse.

www.northlandpub.com

The illustrations were done in pen and ink
with an acrylic wash on watercolor paper.
The text type was set in Janson
The display type was set in Mildew
Composed in the United States of America
Edited by Aimee Jackson
Designed by Jennifer Schaber
Production supervised by Lisa Brownfield

Printed in Hong Kong

10 9 8 7 6 5 4

Adams, Jean Ekman, 1942-
   Clarence goes Out West and meets a purple horse /
written and illustrated by Jean Ekman Adams.
      p. cm.
   Summary: While visiting a western ranch, Clarence the
pig plays cards, line dances, plays the washtub in a cowboy
band, and reads stories at bedtime with his new friend
Smoky the purple horse.
   ISBN 0-87358-753-7
      [1. Pigs–Fiction. 2. Horses–Fiction. 3.
Friendship–Fiction. 4. Ranch life–West
(U.S.)–Fiction. 5. West (U.S.)–Fiction.] I. Title.

PZ7.A2163 C1 2000
[E]–dc21   99-048293